Jetta Dog Finds a Home for Christmas

Story by Kristi Forbes
Pictures by Pooh Day

First Edition

PAGE PUBLISHING, INC.
New York, NY

First originally published by Page Publishing, Inc. 2015

ISBN 978-1-68139-408-4 (pbk)
ISBN 978-1-68139-409-1 (digital)

Printed in the United States of America

For Adrianne Forbes

for bringing Jetta into my life
and for loving and caring for so many
rescue animals.

For Linda Day Duffin

for being my inspiration for everything,
especially to write.

My name is Jetta, and I am a black and gray scrappy little dog with big brown eyes. I am a stray dog in town who lives in North Carolina on the beach. I met a new friend today at the beach named Ms. Annie who is a teacher at one of the schools in town. Ms. Annie asked me to play fetch, and while we were playing, Ms. Annie said my ears are floppy, and when I run, I look like a kangaroo bouncing up and down. Ms. Annie also said when I smile, it looks like I have a huge mustache. She said I am the cutest little dog she has ever seen.

After we finished playing fetch, Ms. Annie asked me, "Are you excited
for Christmas, Jetta, because Christmas is this week?"
I told Ms. Annie, "No, because I do not have a family to spend Christmas with."

Ms. Annie was surprised I did not have a family. I told her my old family had to move to another city and I did not want to go. I wanted to stay here and live at the beach. The beach is my favorite place, but I knew I needed another home, and I wanted another family.

Suddenly, Ms. Annie had a wonderful idea.
She said, "Hop in the car, Jetta. I have a huge surprise for you."

"Where are we going?" I asked.

Ms. Annie said, "We are going to a wonderful place. It's called an animal shelter.
It's a place that helps animals find perfect homes."
Ms. Annie told me there is not any better time to find a family than Christmas.
My heart started beating so fast. I began to get excited at the thought of having a real family to take care of me again, and just in time for Christmas...

We pulled up to the shelter, and I saw an old stone building, but there was the most beautiful painting on the side of the building. It was a painting of all the animals who found families… large dogs, small dogs, cats of all sizes and colors, and even a scrappy-looking dog like me. I asked Ms. Annie, "Did all those animals find homes?"

"Yes," Ms. Annie answered, "and so will you, Jetta."

I walked up to the door, a little scared…Would the other animals like me? Would it be a friendly place? My heart was beating so fast I could hardly breathe, both with excitement and happiness that this could finally be the place where I find a real family of my own!

I opened the door slowly…It was quiet at first, but then *one* bark, *two* barks, *three*, *one* meow, *two* meows, *three*…All at once, everyone was saying hello to me!

Ms. Annie and I met a nice lady at the front counter who said,

“Hello, Annie, who is your friend?”

Ms. Annie said, “This is Jetta, and she’s come here to find a family for Christmas.”

The lady said, “Nice to meet you, Jetta. You are in the right place to find a family. All the dogs stay together in one place, each with their own comfy crate. This is your temporary home over here. I hope you like it.”

I walked over to a group of dogs all playing together and said, "Hi everyone. My name is Jetta. I'm new to the shelter and have come here to find a family."

All the dogs stopped playing and looked up at me. No one was speaking. My heart began to beat faster. I was beginning to think no one liked me and maybe

Then, all of a sudden, a tall, white, strong-looking dog with brown spots walked up to me. My heart was really beating fast now. The strong dog said in a very deep voice, "Hi, Ms. Jetta, I'm Buddy. I am an American bulldog and the leader of this pack, and we are very happy to have you join us."

My heart stopped beating with fear and began to beat with joy. My tail started wagging so fast I could hardly control it.

"Hi, hi, hi, Buddy. How did you get here, and is this a nice place?"

Buddy spoke again very calmly in his deep voice and said, "I love to run, and one day, I saw a squirrel and chased it. Then I kept running. Before I knew it, I had lost my way back home. A very nice lady picked me up and brought me here to the shelter so I can have a nice, warm place to stay. Now, I am waiting for a new family to come adopt me."

Buddy then called the rest of his friends over to meet me.

“This is Annabelle. She is very sweet.”

Annabelle slowly walked over, her head hanging low. She was also tall, but very thin, with big light-brown eyes and long eyelashes. Her fur is yellowish brown, and her tail is wagging very slowly.

Buddy turned to Annabelle and said, “Quit being so shy, Annabelle. Come meet our new friend, Jetta.”

Annabelle walked up to me and said in a very soft voice, “Hi, I’m Annabelle. I’m a golden lab. I grew very tall and got too big for my family’s house, so I came here to find a new family.”

Buddy then said to me, “Meet the last two members of the gang. They are always together. They never go anywhere without each other. This is Fred, and this is Ethyl.”

Fred is very short and chunky, mostly brown with white fur mixed in. His fur is short and ears are floppy. Fred stumbled over to me and slowly said in a deep voice, “Hi, Jetta. I’m Fred and this is Ethyl.”

“Hi, hi, hi, Fred and Ethyl. So nice to meet you,” I said.

Ethyl looked the other way, ignoring everyone. Fred then said, “Ethyl and I grew up together. We are beagles, and we are hunting dogs. We have the best bark in town. We are older now and got tired of hunting, so we came here to find a family and settle down.” Ethyl was still not looking at anyone.

“Ethyl, stop being so unfriendly and come meet Jetta,” Fred said. Ethyl swayed over slowly. She has long soft brown and black fur. Her legs are also very short, but thin. She batted her big dark-brown eyes at me and said, “Hello, you’re very lucky to meet me.”

“Oh, Ethyl,” Fred said. “Be nice to Jetta.”

Ethyl calmly said, “Nice to meet you, Jetta,” and then swayed off, looking at herself in the mirror.

“Ethyl is very pretty, and she knows it,” Buddy said.

I got so excited, I began to jump up and down...I loved my new friends, and I liked it here. What a great place to stay while we all waited to meet our new families.

All of the sudden, the front door opened, and the entire group began to bark with excitement. Buddy told me, "This is one of the best parts of being here."
Then, a very sweet-looking girl walked in. She had beautiful curly golden hair. She had a large bag of treats in her hand.

Buddy said, "This is Adrianne. She is a volunteer and comes here three times a week to walk us, play with us, and give us treats. She is really nice and so much fun to be with."

Adrianne walked over to me and said, "Hello. We have a new friend in our group. What is your name?"

I looked up at Adrianne and knew exactly what Buddy was talking about. She was very sweet and very pretty.

"Hi, hi, hi, my name is Jetta," I said.

"Well, hello, Jetta," Adrianne said, "and here is a treat for you…and for you, Buddy…*and* you, Annabelle…*and* you, Fred, and even you, Ethyl, Ms. Prissy."

After eating our treats, we were so excited we all sprinted outdoors to run and play with Adrianne in an open field with a fence and lots of toys. Buddy told me two guys' names Mike and Bill built this fence for us, and now we have our own fun place to play every day.

We all started to get tired from playing so much, so Adrianne walked us back inside. She cuddled each of us before putting us in our crates, with kisses. Then she said, “I will be back to see you all again soon.”
We barked a *big thank you* to Adrianne. We can’t wait to see her again.

The lights went dim as I looked at all my new friends. I can’t help but say, “I had a wonderful day!”

Then, before I knew it. It was morning. As my eyes were beginning to open, I was still a little tired. I looked out of the window to see a beautiful sunrise, thinking today is the day before Christmas and the day we may all meet our new families.

All of the sudden, Buddy barked out,

“Time to get up everyone! Today is a big day.”

Annabelle lifted her head and said good morning everyone. Fred and Ethyl begin to stir. Fred stumbled out of his crate, and Ethyl waited for him to open the door for her. They all said good morning, ate their breakfast, and then began to get ready for their big day.

FRED

Buddy said to me, "Today is the busiest day of the year at the animal shelter. So many people visit Christmas Eve, looking for a new pet to adopt and bring home to their family, just in time for Christmas."

I suddenly had a *great* idea, so I started calling all of my new friends over.

"Hi, hi, hi everyone…I have a great idea. I bet everyone has a special trick they can do. When someone comes in that looks like a good family for you, begin to do a trick, and then, they will see how great you are."

Buddy loved the idea, and so did Annabelle and Fred. Even Ethyl was excited. "Now everyone choose the one trick you do best and practice," I said. So they all began to practice.

Buddy can **throw** a ball in the air and balance it right on the tip of his nose. Annabelle is tall and can **leap** high almost over anything. Fred can **sing** the most beautiful song in a very low voice. Ethyl can do the most graceful **ballet** dance. And I can **balance** on my two back feet and stand up straight bouncing around in circles.

Everyone began to bark and howl with joy. We all knew that now, we would surely find a family when we show them our special tricks.

Soon the door opened, and a tall strong-looking boy walked in. He had a big smile on his face and looked really smart. Everyone looked over at Buddy and said, "He is perfect for you, Buddy…Hurry and show him your special trick."

Buddy's heart was beating with more excitement than ever before. He began to bounce his ball right on the tip of his nose.

The boy walked over to Buddy. **"Hi, what's your name?"** the boy asked, rubbing Buddy between his ears. Buddy barked out his name, and the boy said, "I love to play ball. It's my favorite sport. I can throw the ball to you, and you can catch it and balance it on your nose. Let's give it a try."

The boy threw the ball, and Buddy caught it perfectly, bounced it, then balanced it on the tip of his nose, the best he had ever done.

The boy was so excited he hugged Buddy and said the **magic words,** "Would you like to go home with me for Christmas and be a part of our family?"

Buddy jumped in the boy's arms and was so happy. He had found his family. The boy put him down so he could walk over to everyone to tell them good-bye.

"I am so happy," he said. "I will miss you all, but we will see each other again soon. We can all meet at Jetta's favorite place, the beach."

Everyone began to jump up and down with such excitement for Buddy. They all waved good-bye as Buddy walked out the door, **wagging his tail like never before!**

Just then, the door opened again, and a very tall, sweet-looking somewhat shy girl walks in. She had golden-looking hair that looked exactly like Annabelle's. I looked over at Annabelle and said,

"Annabelle, do your trick now."

Annabelle stood up tall and got a running start to leap right over the crates and land right in front of the girl, perfectly.

The girl looked up slowly at Annabelle and said, "Hi, what is your name?" Annabelle barked out her name. The girl said, "We have the same color hair, and I love to jump. It is my favorite thing to do. We can play and jump together!"

They both began to jump over the crates. Then, the girl looked down at Annabelle and said the **magic words**, "Would you like to go home with me for Christmas and **be a part of our family?"**

Annabelle could hardly stay calm. She was so happy. She barked a *big yes* and jumped right into the girl's arms. Annabelle looked at all her friends and said, "Good-bye, I will see you again soon when we all meet at the beach."

Everyone was so happy for Annabelle and waved good-bye as Annabelle walked out the door, **wagging her tail like never before.**

"Well," I said, "it's just me and you two, Fred and Ethyl. Let's go stand back by our crates and wait for someone else to come in. This has been a *great day!*"

Slowly, the front door opened again. A nice-looking older couple walked in. They looked like someone's grandmother and grandfather. Both are very short. The man had a funny grin, and the lady had the most beautiful eyes that sparkled, and her smile was so cute.

I looked over at Fred and Ethyl and said, **"They are perfect for you! Do your tricks quickly."**

Fred began to sing "Rudolph the Red-Nosed Reindeer" in his deepest clearest voice, and Ethyl began to dance her ballet to Fred's song. They looked as if they were performing in a concert and they performed their tricks perfectly.

The older couple began to walk over to Fred and Ethyl. They leaned down and asked them their names, stroking them both gently. Fred barked out his name before they could hardly finish asking, and then they both looked over at Ethyl. She looked away. Fred got very worried. This was not the time for Ethyl to be unfriendly! But all of the sudden, Ethyl barked out the most beautiful bark ever and jumped right in the lady's arms.

The lady said, **"I love the ballet. I used to be a ballerina. We can do ballet together."**

The man looked over at Fred and said, "My favorite thing to do is sing. I sing all the time, and my favorite songs to sing are Christmas songs."

The man and lady looked down at Fred and Ethyl and said the **magic words, "Would you like to go home with us for Christmas and be a part of our family?"**

Fred and Ethyl were so happy. They had found the perfect family, both of them together and just in time for Christmas!

I was so happy for them. I walked over and said, "Merry Christmas, Fred! Merry Christmas, Ethyl! I can't wait to see you again soon. Don't forget we will all meet at the beach." Fred and Ethyl said good-bye to me and walked out the door, **wagging both their tails like never before.**

I stood there all alone. All of my friends had found a home. I was happy for them, but the day was almost over. No one else was coming in. It was quiet and almost Christmas. Everyone was getting the shelter ready for the close of the day by setting food and water for me. I stood by my crate, staring at the door. The sun was going down, and all the staff and volunteers were getting ready to go home.

"Good night, Jetta," someone yelled out.

"Merry Christmas," someone else yelled out. "See you in two days."

They started turning out the lights. I felt alone. Was no one else coming? How could the day end without me finding a family?

"Good night. Good night. Merry Christmas," I called out.

Just then, I saw lights shining through the window. I heard a door slam and then another door opened. I lifted my head and heard the sweetest voice ever. **"Are you closed?"**

"Almost," the manager of the shelter said. "You can come on in, but hurry, it is Christmas Eve, you know, and I have to get home to my family."

"Okay, we won't be long!" a kind voice yelled out.

I looked around the corner and saw a young couple walking in. The woman had a gentle smile, and the man had a twinkle in his eyes. They both seemed so friendly. The young woman called out,

"Is anyone left in the shelter?"

I stood up quickly. My heart was beating so fast. I let out a very loud bark and began to bounce around excitedly on my two hind legs, longer than I had ever done before.

In a soft voice the woman said,

"Look at you, what is your name?"

"Jetta," I barked as loud as I could.

The woman said, "Jetta is standing tall on her hind legs and looks just like a person."

The young man said, "Yes, and she has black curly and gray hair just like me."

"Hi there, Ms. Jetta. We are all alone in a great house with a large backyard. We thought we would make a visit to the animal shelter in hopes of finding a special pet to take home with us for Christmas."

My heart was really beating fast now. Do they like me? Could they really be this perfect? Would I finally find my family tonight on Christmas Eve?

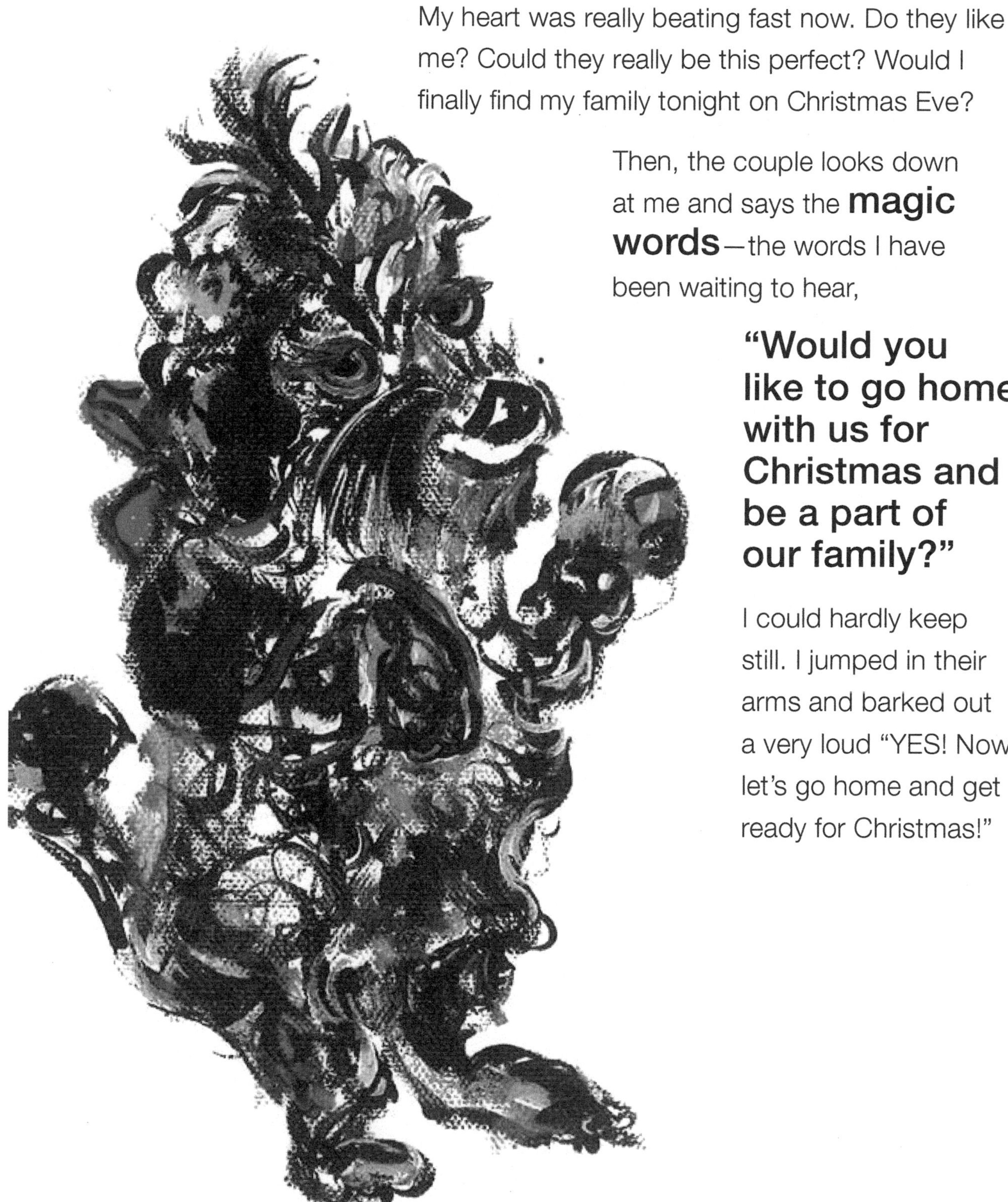

Then, the couple looks down at me and says the **magic words**—the words I have been waiting to hear,

"Would you like to go home with us for Christmas and be a part of our family?"

I could hardly keep still. I jumped in their arms and barked out a very loud "YES! Now let's go home and get ready for Christmas!"

The three of us walk out the door, and I am wagging my tail like never before!

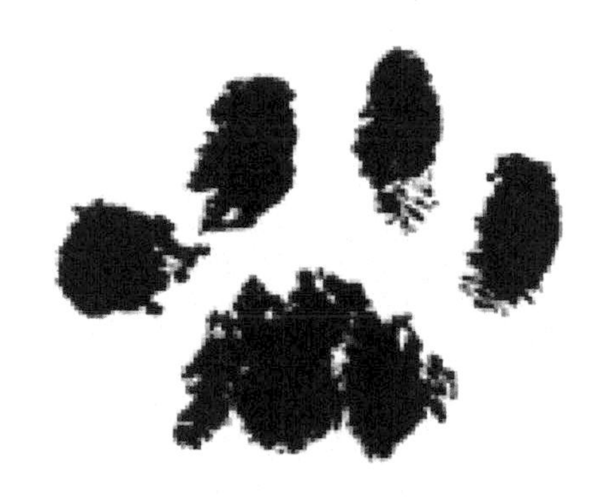

The end!
Or just the beginning?

About the Author

When I look out at my backyard today, I see my wonderful husband and amazing dog Jetta surrounded by hummingbirds, Peachtree streets, and city lights. The backyard of my growing-up years was a strip of land called Radio Island in North Carolina. Situated between two bridges with seagulls, the ocean, and sand dunes, it is a place where books are written about, people dream to visit and friends and family (including furry children) are priorities. I attended college in North Carolina at East Carolina University and moved to Atlanta over twenty years ago for an internship and never left. I love Atlanta and city living. This book originated from the happiness brought to us by a little furry four-legged family member. Jetta has added so much love to my family, and I hope her stories will do the same for my readers.

CPSIA information can be obtained at www.ICGtesting.com
Printed in the USA
LVOW05s1057290715
448075LV00003B/3/P